# We Love the Seashore

Library of Congress Control Number: 2006038439

ISBN 978 1 59566 369 6

Written by Kate Tym
Edited by Clare Weaver
Designed by Alix Wood
Illustrated by Jana Christy
Consultancy by Anne Faundez

Publisher Steve Evans
Creative Director Zeta Davies
Senior Editor Hannah Ray

Printed and bound in China

# We Love the Seashore

Kate Tym

Illustrated by Jana Christy

QEB Publishing

We wake up in the morning
And it's a sunny day.
Mommy grabs the cooler,
And we know just what she'll say:

"Get your things together kids,
Swimsuits, towels, and inflatable rings;
Buckets, shovels, and sunhats.
All your seashore things."

We take sandwiches and oranges,
Chips and apple juice,
Sunscreen and flip-flops,
And Billy's squeaky moose.

We take a floatie and umbrella,
Bananas and a cake,
A blanket and some sausages,
And a new, red plastic rake.

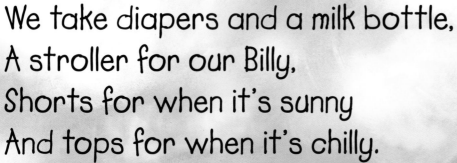

We take diapers and a milk bottle,
A stroller for our Billy,
Shorts for when it's sunny
And tops for when it's chilly.

There's Mom and Dad up front,
In the middle, Bill and Molly.
Then Stan and Ella in the back
With Ella's favorite dolly.

We sing songs and eat some snacks,
And Molly plays I Spy.

Stan starts bugging Ella,
And even makes her cry.

We feel all hot and horrible,
Sticky, bored, and rotten.
But once we get to the seashore,
All of that's forgotten.

We pile out of the car
And race across the sand,
Ella, Stan, and Molly
Holding Billy by the hand.

We dig moats and make sandcastles,
Which we decorate with shells.
We find oysters and a starfish
And an old, dead crab that smells.

Stan and Molly go swimming,
Splashing madly in the water,

While Daddy plays "jump-wave"
With his younger son and daughter.

We find rock pools and seaweed,
And a lot of sand to sprinkle.
Billy takes his diaper off
for an outside, seashore tinkle.

We play baseball and frisbee,
Catch, and have a race.
Then, we bury Daddy in the sand,
Right up to his face.

Mommy rubs on sunscreen
And says, "Keep your hats on!"
She hands out the sandwiches,
Some of which Billy sat on.

Mommy feeds Billy
And Daddy helps feed Molly,
Billy feeds squeaky moose,
And Ella feeds her dolly.

Then it's time for ice cream.
A yummy cone for Stan
And sticky orange lollies,
All melting from the van.

Dripping over fingers,
Drooling down our faces,
Mommy gets the wipes out
And cleans our sticky places.

Mommy hates a mess.
It really makes her mad.
She always wipes everything.
She even wipes Dad!

And then lunch is over.
Each has had their share.
Billy's eaten pebbles,
But no one seems to care.

The fun fair awaits us
With its music, sounds, and sights.
People screaming, horns blaring,
And loads of flashing lights.

There's a carousel and games,
A spooky fortune-teller,
A helter-skelter and ghost train,
And a ride called "Inter-Stellar."

There are doughnuts and cotton candy,
Sweet treats for our tummies,
Little children going around and around,
And waving at their mommies.

Dad goes on the "Caterpillar,"
A roller coaster ride,
But says he won't go on again

—he's feeling odd inside.

Mom and Stan go on the "Slammer,"
And Dad can hardly look.

He takes Molly, Bill, and Ella
On the little "Babbling Brook."

Then it's onto the games machines.
There's so much to be won,

Billy's got four prizes.
The rest of
us have none!

Then we stop for hot dogs
With onions and some sauce,
And a little something for after...
Pink cotton candy, of course!

We head back to the parking lot,
But Billy's acting hyper.
We buy him a swirling windmill
And stop to change his diaper.

Before we're out of the parking lot,
Billy's fast asleep.
We're all tired, but glowing
With the memory that we'll keep

Of our day at the beach,
Throwing pebbles by the shore.
And next time we're on vacation,
We'll all be back for more!

# Notes for Teachers and Parents

- Play a game of I Spy with the children, like Molly in the story. Say "I spy, with my little eye, something beginning with..." and pick the letter your object begins with. Discuss letter sounds with the children. We can hear that "hat" begins with an "h" sound. Once the children have mastered single letter sounds, try conjoined sounds. For example, "shell" begins with an "s," but the sound it starts with is formed by an "s" and "h" joined together to make a "sh" sound. Also, try two words at a time. For example, "street light" begins with "s" and "l." To make the game fun for younger children, you can adapt it to use description, rather than letter sounds. For example, "I spy, with my little eye, something that is green and brown and has leaves". A tree!

- Plan a beach-style picnic with the children. Talk about all the things you'll need. Write a list. Encourage the children to wear their sun hats, sunscreen, and sunglasses. Talk about why they need to do this. The children can draw their favorite foods on white paper plates and lay them out around a picnic blanket. Why not get out the cooler and have a real picnic, too!

- Build a fun fair using materials such as cereal boxes, cardboard tubes, egg cartons, yogurt cups, and aluminum foil. The children can make the rides mentioned in the story

- Play the seashore memory game. The first player says: "I went to the seashore and I brought...an umbrella." The second player has to repeat the sentence, remember the first object, and add another to the list. For example: "I went to the seashore and brought an umbrella and...a bikini." The third player has to remember the first two items and add a third, and so on. Continue until the list is so long that the children can't remember any more items.

- Encourage the children to make a seashore picture. Talk about all the things you can see at the shore and, using pens, paints, crayons, and tissue paper, make a beautiful beach collage. Use shiny paper or aluminum foil for the sea. Use real sand for the beach. Collect feathers to make sea gulls. Let the children's imaginations run wild.

- Help the children make windmills. Using stiff, colored paper, draw a square, and then make cuts from the corners to just short of the center. Bend alternate points to the center and fasten to a drinking straw with a split pin.

- Ask the children to paint pebbles. Stones provide really nice, smooth surfaces for painting and they are a great reminder of a day at the beach. When they're competely dry, the painted stones can be varnished and used as paperweights.